THE KAMA SUTRA

ANNE HOOPER

THE KAMA SUTRA

ANNE HOOPER

DORLING KINDERSLEY

London • New York • Sydney

www.dk.com

A DORLING KINDERSLEY BOOK

www.dk.com

Designed and edited by
Focus Publishing

Senior Managing Art Editor	Lynne Brown
Senior Managing Editor	Corinne Roberts
Senior Art Editor	Karen Ward
Project Editor	Claire Cross
DTP	Rajen Shah
Production	Martin Croshaw

This edition published in 2003 by
Dorling Kindersley Limited,
80 Strand, London, WC2R ORL

A CIP catalogue record for this book is
available from the British Library

ISBN 0–7513–0799–8

Reproduced by GRB Editrice Srl. Italy
Printed in Singapore by Star Standard

CONTENTS

Introduction 6

Preparing for Love 12

Touching and Caressing 34

Kissing 54

Kama Sutra Positions 78

Ananga Ranga Positions 140

Perfumed Garden Positions 182

Before and After Love 210

Index 237

Acknowledgments 240

INTRODUCTION

Sales of Tantric sex books are staggering — obviously the world remains fascinated by the idea of having sex for hours in a state of ecstasy! To feed the public hunger for this disciplined/spiritual approach to sex, I have been asked to write this gorgeous-to-hold-in-the-hand, tactile version of my *Kama Sutra*, based on the principles of Tantric sex.

So what exactly is it about the *Kama Sutra* that catches the public imagination at a time in history when people care more about their Sunday trip to the supermarket than their soul? Make no mistake. The Tantric disciplines that lie behind the *Kama Sutra* are taken seriously. There is a great swathe of men and women looking for meaning in their lives, and it is here that I believe the secret of the *Kama Sutra's* success lies.

SEX AND SPIRITUALITY

As we become more divorced from contemplation and increasingly urbanized, we no longer experience the simple (but vital) joys of the seasons. We don't delight

in the renewal of spring any longer for the good reason
that we don't know it's there. The only time we bask in
the sunshine is on our annual vacation to Mexico or
Ibiza. The reason these things matter is because this
was how we used to experience a sense of spirituality,
a sense of rhythm, a deeper knowledge
that time is passing. The seasons are
markers of the stages of our own
lives. Without such markers, it gets
harder to put our own struggles and
achievements into contexts. So
we look for other ways of
doing it. Sex is, perhaps,
one of the last great natural
joys, available both to
prince and pauper. It is real,
it is close; above everything
else, it offers meaning
to life.

This is where the *Kama Sutra* comes in. For behind the challenging sex positions, the flowery titles to the poses, the original archaic language, lies the promise of discovering pure spirituality within oneself. It is a spirituality that has been present all the time, only we never knew it.

The Eastern attitude to sex is not only open but life-enhancing, and it is unlike the culture most of us in the West were brought up with. Sex is seen not just as a bodily function but as something which very occasionally gives us glimpses of heaven. Tantric sex theorizes that, through sex, we can experience expanded and enhanced being; it heightens and prolongs the special rapport that exists between a man and a woman while making love. The point of a Tantric sex program is to aim consciously at merging yourself ecstatically with your partner and, through him or her, with the rest of the world. In this new edition of the *Kama Sutra* we include, for the first time, a three-day Tantric sex program, simple to follow; at its most relaxed, it offers pleasant companionship; at its best, the experience of sex as if you were each other.

PUTTING THE *KAMA SUTRA* INTO CONTEXT

Of course the original version of the *Kama Sutra*, written by Vatsyayana in the 4th Century AD and translated by the Victorian explorer Sir Richard Burton, was produced for men. But it was written to assist men give their women a wonderful experience in bed. Vatsyayana was a man of his times and believed that life consisted of *dharma*, *artha*, and *kama*. Dharma was the acquisition of religious merit; artha was the acquisition of wealth; and kama was the acquisition of love or sensual pleasure. The *Kama Sutra* was conceived, therefore, as a kind of businessmen's textbook. I have attempted in the previous versions and in this one to combine the fascinating and still highly relevant information offered by Vatsyayana with contemporary explanation. By putting the sex tips and sexual positions into the context of the 21st century, I've tried to give his archaic advice meaning for all of us today.

Of course, the main social change between India in the 4th century and much of the world now is in the status of women. If you attempted to publish a sex book today that regarded women as having no power over their lives, you would probably be lynched. Therefore, in this edition I have deliberately included information for women that doesn't exist in the original version of the *Kama Sutra*, but that clearly acknowledges that women are on very much of a sexual par with their men.

ANANGA RANGA

Two years after the publication of the *Kama Sutra*, Sir Richard Burton went on to produce the first Western edition of the *Ananga Ranga*. The *Ananga Ranga* is a collection of erotic works, including details from the *Kama Sutra*, specifically aimed at preventing the separation of husband and wife. The book appeared around the start of the Crusades — a time of great cultural exchange between East and West.

THE PERFUMED GARDEN

This book was the third of Sir Richard Burton's publications for the Victorian Kama Shastra Society, which translated rare and important texts concerned with love and sex. The original text of *The Perfumed Garden* included a large section on homosexual practices which Burton diligently translated. However, after Burton's death, his wife, who did not approve of her husband's work, threw the new translation into the fire. However, fortunately all was not lost, because Burton's friend and colleague, Dr. Grenfell Baker, managed to reproduce much of the material from conversations he had had with Burton before his death.

Preparing
for Love

CHOOSING A MATE

Vatsyayana lists an array of skills he deems essential to anyone wanting to be taken seriously in the game of love. Since these include talents as diverse as "playing on musical glasses full of water" and having a "knowledge of mines and quarries," modern readers may find some of his advice irrelevant. However, the *Kama Sutra* also contains a number of insights that do still apply today. For instance, Vatsyayana tells us that a woman who "likes the same things that the man likes, and who has the power to attract the minds of others" is more likely to be successful in winning over the man of her choice. Modern psychological research into the factors that influence compatibility and attractiveness backs up this contention. The possession of similar backgrounds and interests is definitely the best guarantee of relationship success. In the highly stratified world of ancient India, this meant that men and women could only marry within their caste. Similarly, in the West today, your most compatible partner is still likely to come from within your own social group.

Getting to Know One Another

At a time when all marriages were arranged, men and women were spared the tricky initial stages of forming a relationship. Today, meeting a new person, deciding that you like them, and getting off on the right foot are more difficult. Vatsyayana constantly assumes that the man is always in the dominant role. He talks of "winning over" the woman, and says that the man should "make use of those devices by which he can establish himself more into her confidence." Sound advice, but advice that now applies to both sexes.

LOVE AND MARRIAGE

Even in the 4th century AD some people believed that men should follow their hearts. Vatsyayana tells us: "...prosperity is gained only by marrying that girl to whom one becomes attached..."

21ST CENTURY ADVICE

Warmth, a positive approach, and tenderness are
essential in creating the right impression. Positive
signals, such as establishing eye contact, or emulating
and responding to the other person's body language,
show that you are open, friendly, and eager.

However, building a relationship is about more than
simple tricks of body language. Prospective partners
need to give one another genuine, positive feedback
and reassurance. Listen carefully and be genuine and
open in return. Only in an atmosphere of trust and
reciprocation can a worthwhile relationship develop.

Dating

*B*uilding an intimate and loving relationship is an exciting and enjoyable process. But it can also be difficult if you have to juggle a burgeoning romance with a heavy workload and the demands of friends and family. On the one hand a relationship can quickly go cool if you don't invest sufficient time and energy. On the other, trying to accelerate things to make up for a lack of time can lead to premature or forced intimacy.

In the *Kama Sutra*, Vatsyayana paints a picture of the social life of a typical "citizen" of the 4th century – a social life intriguingly familiar to the modern reader. There were relaxed evenings with friends where new acquaintances would be entertained with "loving and agreeable conversation"; parties, complete with party games such as "the completion of verses… and the testing of knowledge"; and even picnics and drinking nights. All were recommended as good places to get to know the object of your affection in a relaxed and nonpressurized way. Basically, the intention was that the couple could begin their "dating" in the supportive atmosphere of their social network.

NURTURE YOUR RELATIONSHIP TODAY

Admittedly the *Kama Sutra* was intended for high caste
readers, with a good standard of living and a lots of
leisure time. But the guidelines it sets out are still valid
today. New relationships need to be nurtured in a warm,
supportive environment, and integrating your social life
with your love life, to at least some degree, can both
alleviate time pressures and help you to satisfy the
demands of friends and lovers. Once the relationship
has been satisfactorily established within an overall social
context, then the couple can move comfortably to more
private trysts, just as in 4th century India.

Social Behavior

During the 4th century Indian men and women had well-defined sexual roles to play, roles laid down by a resolutely patriarchal society. These rules sometimes involved a distinct double standard. For instance, men were expected to have as much sexual experience as possible, while a woman had to be a virgin at marriage or else be ruled out of decent society.

Similar attitudes prevailed in the West until only a few decades ago, and continue to predominate in most of the rest of the world. However, the sexual revolution has brought about a reassessment of some of the assumptions associated with these social constraints.

SEX AND CASTE

The rigid social stratification of 4th century India placed its own constraints on the possible choice of sexual partners: "The practice of Kama with women of the higher castes is prohibited ... Amusement in society should be carried on only with our equals."

For instance, it is now seen to be natural and desirable for women to be sexually assertive — indeed many men complain that their wives or girlfriends are too reluctant to take the lead.

SEX EDUCATION THEN AND NOW

One way in which Vatsyayana displayed an admirably enlightened view was his insistence that sexual education is essential for both men and women: "A female, therefore, should learn the *Kama Shastra*" [the science of sex]. Actually talking and reading about sexuality is one of the great advances for would-be loving couples, and progress in recent decades means that Vatsyayana's wise advice now generally holds sway.

Preparing the Mind

*T*he *Kama Sutra* adopts a very holistic approach to sex, covering every aspect of the erotic, from the correct social niceties to recipes for aphrodisiacs. Naturally, Vatsyayana did not neglect the most important erogenous zone of them all – the mind.

"Kama," he tells us, "is the enjoyment of appropriate objects by the five senses, assisted by the mind together with the soul."

Great sex begins in the head. You need to be relaxed yet aroused – romantic and passionate at the same time. Getting physically and mentally in the mood is all about preparing your mind properly, and the *Kama Sutra* is quite specific about the sorts of things you can do, from gentle touching to suggestive conversation.

PUT YOUR PARTNER AT EASE

However, Vatsyayana's advice is about much more than simply talking suggestively to the object of your desire. By putting your partner at ease, you provide a secure atmosphere in which the two of you can communicate freely, relaxing enough to really let go in bed. Vatsyayana knew that an unappealing environment was a sure-fire turn off. He advised that the "pleasure room" should be decorated with flowers and perfumed with beautiful fragrances, while the bed should be covered with "a clean, white cloth and strewn with flowers and garlands" – a gorgeous idea for today!

Preparing the Body

The Hindu tradition that produced the *Kama Sutra* saw the human body as a vehicle for expressing spirituality — not, as in the West for many centuries since, as a sinful thing. Sex is celebrated as a sacrament, and the erotic statues and wall carvings seen in Hindu temples throughout India pay testimony to this ancient belief.

The Hindu tradition regards the body as deserving of being treated with reverence, and in the section describing the "life of a citizen," the *Kama Sutra* details the care it should receive: "Now the house-holder, having got up in the morning and performed his necessary duties, should wash his teeth, apply a limited quantity of ointments and perfumes to his body, put some ornaments on his person and *collyrium* [a medicated eye lotion] on his eyelids and below his eyes, color his lips with *alacktaka* [a dye], and look at himself in the glass. Having then eaten betel leaves, with other things that give fragrance to the mouth, he should perform his usual business. He should bathe daily, anoint his body with oil every other day, apply a lathering substance to his body every three days, get his head (including face) shaved every four days, and the other parts of his body every five or ten days. All these things should be done without fail, and the sweat of the armpits should also be removed."

Be sure that what you use on your hair and body appeals not just to you but to your partner, too. Whether you are male or female, a fragrance that does not suit you will probably turn your lover off.

Cultural preferences change, and the details are not as important as the principle. Two thousand years later, cleanliness remains a priority for nearly all lovers, and for many the use of fragrances enhances lovemaking.

Erogenous Zones

S ome say that the most potent sexual organ of all is the brain. The most obvious meaning of this wise dictum is that, without the free play of the imagination, sex can become a soulless and mechanical activity. Male or female, what good lovers have in common is a sensitive and imaginative appreciation of those parts of the body that are rather clinically referred to as the erogenous zones. Perhaps we should call these the pleasure zones, for it is by tapping their erotic potential that you can complement the more extreme joys of which the body is capable. No one who is sexually active would deny that the genitals are one of the primary erogenous zones, along with the brain and the skin. But to concentrate on them to the exclusion of the body's myriad other pleasure zones is like eating part of a good meal and leaving the rest.

The classic books on Eastern sexual practice share an awareness of the pleasure zones. They speak of these in terms of kissing and touching. Of the kiss, for example, the *Kama Sutra* says that the places where it should be applied include the lips, the inside of the mouth, the forehead, the cheeks, the throat, and the breasts. Most of us also appreciate the potential for pleasure in the nipples, the buttocks, the earlobes, and the feet. The list is as long as you want it to be; find the zones that give you both the most pleasure.

More Erogenous Zones

*T*he skin is the largest organ of the human body, richly endowed with sensitive nerve endings that respond to the lightest touch and the smallest changes in temperature or pressure. For example, on average there are about 1,500 sensory receptors, including touch-sensitive nerve endings, in every square inch of a typical woman's skin. The skin's sensitivity to stimuli varies from one part of the body to another, and the

erogenous zones are among the areas that are especially sensitive to touch. In these areas, sensitivity really is the watchword: the slightest touch can induce an effect.

Among the most sensitive areas on any woman's body are the breasts. A woman's breasts play a major role in sexual attraction. Woman is the only primate female who has swollen mammary glands when she is not producing milk, which highlights the role of the breasts as being more than simply a means of feeding her young. In addition to serving to attract the male, the breasts are undeniably one of the most significant pleasure zones.

The nipples and the surrounding areas (the areolae) are highly sensitive to touch, and some women can reach orgasm by stimulation of the nipples alone.

Creating the Mood

Just as it is important to prepare the body for love, so you should pay careful attention to creating an ambience that is conducive to lovemaking before you actually begin. Now, as in the time of the *Kama Sutra*, the way a couple feels about the prevailing mood and surrounding environment for lovemaking is of prime importance, and there are a number of things you can do to create the right atmosphere.

It is a good idea to provide background music that enhances the mood — neither too raucous nor agitated, as this will not be conducive to a tender exchange, nor too soporific, which will make you feel sleepy. Tastes in music vary widely, but it is important to choose something that makes you and your partner feel relaxed and at the same time alert and attentive to each other. Naturally you will not want to be disturbed, so if you do not have an answering machine, it may be best to unplug the phone.

Finally, sexual passion and overindulgence in food and drink may be linked in the popular image of the complete sensualist, but in practice the combination seldom works. While it is often tempting to preface your lovemaking with a lavish meal, or even worse, with a surfeit of alcohol, neither will do anything for you and your partner. Try not to overdo things as you get "in the mood." Lovemaking is usually best on a satisfied but not overfull stomach, and certainly with a clear head, for you will never attain the enjoyment and satisfaction you seek if either of you is in discomfort or falling asleep through the effects of overindulgence. Save yourselves for the act of lovemaking itself.

The Setting for Love

When preparing for lovemaking, make sure that in cold weather the room is warm enough (but not stuffy), and that in hot weather it is refreshingly cool. Despite the differences between the modern world and the India of the *Kama Sutra*, we could do worse than to follow the advice of Vatsyayana, who tells us that the room should be: "balmy with rich perfumes, should contain a bed, soft, agreeable to the sight, covered with a clean white cloth, low in the middle part, having garlands and bunches of flowers upon it, and a canopy above it, and two pillows, one at the top, another at the bottom. There should also be a sort of couch besides, and at the head of this a sort of stool, on which should be placed the fragrant ointments for the night, as well as flowers, pots containing *collyrium* and other fragrant substances, things used for perfuming the mouth, and the bark of the common citron tree."

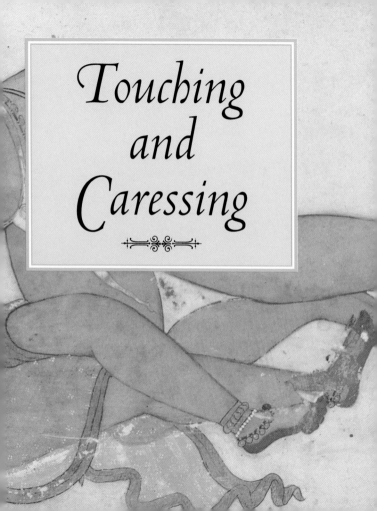

Touching
and
Caressing

❖❖❖

EMBRACING LOVE

A discussion of embracing – or indeed many different forms of touching and caressing – is central to the *Kama Sutra*. Vatsyayana begins by dividing the embrace into eight kinds, which form two groups of four. The first group indicates "the mutual love of a man and woman who have come together," and the second, embraces that occur "at the time of the meeting." The latter group includes the Twining of a Creeper and the Milk and Water Embrace, both of which are featured in the following pages.

In addition to the eight basic embraces, Vatsyayana lists "four ways of embracing simple members of the body" – these "simple members" being the thighs, the jaghana (the middle part of the body), the breasts, and the forehead.

In describing these embraces, Vatsyayana was probably just categorizing observed behavior rather than giving practical instruction. In the same way, he goes on to consider the importance of mutual grooming as preparation for lovemaking, and scratching and hair play as pleasurable alternatives to standard embracing.

The Twining of a Creeper

“*This embrace occurs when a woman, clinging to a man as a creeper twines round a tree, bends his head down to hers with the desire of kissing him and slightly makes the sound of* sut sut — *it is like the twining of a creeper.*”

FROM THIS description, it appears that Vatsyayana assumed the woman would be shorter than the man, which was probably as common in his time as it is today. The *sut sut* to which he refers is his way of trying to put inarticulate sounds into words.

The Milk and Water Embrace

"When a man and a woman are very much in love with each other, and, not thinking of any pain or hurt, embrace each other as if they were entering into each other's bodies either while the woman is sitting on the lap of the man, or in front of him, or on a bed, then it is called an embrace like a mixture of milk and water."

THE MILK AND WATER EMBRACE has a name evocative of a total mingling, and it graphically describes how lovers try to lose themselves in each other, especially early on in their physical relationship.

Mutual Grooming

"It is recommended that a man shave no more often than every four days. But a woman will most likely prefer not to be grazed by her partner's growth when he kisses her. As an alternative to asking him to shave before making love, she could try shaving him herself. Shaving is not just for men, however, because many women shave their legs and armpits and some shave off their pubic hair; certain men find a hairless pudendum very erotic."

MUTUAL GROOMING
is by no means an
indispensable ritual,
but by delaying the
consummation of love,
and focusing the couple's
attention on each other's
attractions, it can heighten
the anticipation of pleasure.
It also encourages feelings of
tenderness, trust, and caring,
enabling each partner to feel
protective toward the other.
This can help break down
inhibitions in a new
relationship, and will
reinforce the bonds of an
established one. Shaving one
another, or washing each
other's hair, are ideal ways
of enhancing closeness
and trust while
preparing for love.

Sensual Massage

"*For thousands of years, massage has been valued as a means of soothing away tiredness and tension. And yet, because we link touch with sex, we tend to steer clear of touching each other for fear of being misunderstood. This habit can even extend, inappropriately, to our partners, so that we concentrate on purely sexual expression, avoiding any systematic sensual touching. By ignoring the power of massage, many lovers miss out on a source of great pleasure as well as a means of making the body much more receptive and relaxed for lovemaking. Massage the front of the shoulders, the sides of the neck, the cheeks and the jaw, and then the temples and forehead. Run your fingers lightly over the chin and over the lips, eyes, and nose, all of which by now should be pleasantly sensitized. Many people also enjoy having the top of the head massaged, with an action like that used in washing hair.*"

When MASSAGING the back, use gentle, erotic pressure and work upward from the buttocks, keeping your hands outspread and level with each other and your thumbs pushing inward along the spine. Work up to the base of the neck and then out to the shoulders before bringing your hands slowly down the sides to the buttocks. Repeat this massage about ten times.

Basic Massage Strokes

Y ou can learn the essentials of massage fairly quickly, and all of the following actions are recommended for a technique that should enhance your lovemaking experience.

EFFLEURAGE Glide your palms across the skin, putting your body weight behind the movement. This action should be used first and last on each area.

KNEADING With your hands gently curved, knead the flesh with a smooth, regular movement.

PÉTRISSAGE Move the balls of your fingers or thumbs in a circular motion to soothe away any muscular tension along the spine. Do not, however, massage the spine itself.

HACKING Giving a series of brisk chops with the side of the hand – as in karate, but gentler – is refreshing.

TAPOTEMENT AND CUPPING Tapotement involves drumming with a light tapping action. Cupping is pounding the body with alternate hands that are cupped with fingers together and thumbs folded in.

Whichever massage technique or stroke you use, always keep your movements even, rhythmic, and symmetrical, and follow each one through where appropriate. Always use a suitable oil (see below), and agree with your partner on the amount of pressure to be used, since this should always be a matter of pleasure for you both. Also, you should learn to forgo your own needs temporarily and concentrate instead on your partner's enjoyment. By doing so, you will attain the prized goal of being able to give and receive pleasure fully.

You can massage your partner with dry hands, but your movements will be smoother, especially if you are new to it, if you use a massage oil or an oil-free massage lotion. There is a wide variety of nut- and vegetable-based oils available.

More Sensual Massage

"All massage oils work best when they have been prewarmed by rubbing them for a few seconds between the hands. Used cold, they come as a shock to the skin. Oil each area before you attend to it rather than oiling the whole body first: apply a small amount to the part you intend to massage, and rub it into the skin with smooth but firm strokes. After the massage, the oil can be left to soak into the skin."

WITH YOUR PARTNER lying facedown, start by
massaging the toes – stretching, kneading, and
bending each one upward – before softly rubbing
the areas between them. Next, run the palms
of your hands firmly over the soles of the feet
and then along the tops. Raise each leg in turn
and gently rotate each foot a few times until it
feels loose and relaxed. Gradually move up the
leg, paying special attention to the ankles,
calves, and backs of the knees and the thighs.

Scratching

Although lovers often use their fingernails to express passion on parting or meeting, or on reconciliation after a quarrel, pressing and scratching with them during lovemaking can be surprisingly erotic. In many cultures, marks of passion on a young woman's breast or throat serve to tell the world that she is spoken for. Such marks can excite admiration.

IF LEAVING LOVE MARKS is based on passion rather than anger or cruelty, both partners may find it fun from time to time. If you want to try giving your partner loving scratches, first make sure that your nails are clean and free of any jagged edges. Then you can raise short-lived marks on his or her skin without actually cutting it.

You are unlikely to want to use the marks to denote "ownership" of a partner, as in ancient Indian times, so do not be over-zealous in your scratching. If too much pressure is applied, it can be very painful!

Hair Play

*"A woman's hair has eternal fascination for a man.
Among the arts she should learn is that of dressing the hair
with perfumes. The power that her hair exerts is
reciprocated when, by praising and fondling it, her
partner arouses feelings of desire in her, which he
then tries to satisfy."*

LOVING TOUCH is one of the most important parts
of an intimate relationship, and by running his
fingers through his partner's hair while she plays
with his, a man can increase the tactile pleasure for
both of them and generally enhance the mood.

Kissing

KISSING

T he mouth is among the most sensitive parts of the body, and the most versatile — you can use your lips or tongue to kiss, lick, suck, nuzzle, or nibble any area of your partner's body. Kissing is an art in itself, and the *Kama Sutra* recognizes its power of expression by describing in detail the different forms of kissing and when each type of kiss is appropriate. Whatever its intensity, a kiss on the lips combines the three senses of touch, taste, and smell, each of which can produce a strong emotional response. Kisses range from fleeting contact to a deep penetration with the tongue. In between lie many variations, and perhaps the *Kama Sutra* describes types of kisses in such great detail because the skill was just as often overlooked then as it is now.

Vatsyayana rightly portrays kissing as an essential part of foreplay for the accomplished lover. Underlining the importance he grants it, Vatsyayana is as thorough, if not as methodical, in listing the different kinds of kiss as he is in detailing the numerous embraces and lovemaking positions to be found in the *Kama Sutra*.

Sensual Kissing

"The Straight Kiss is the name given to a kiss in which the lips of two lovers are brought into direct contact with each other."

WHEN LOVERS KISS like this, with their heads angled only slightly to each side, tongue penetration is impractical. Because of this, the straight kiss is not a means of expressing intense passion, but it is a gentle way of showing affection and expressing the initial stages of desire. It's the kind of kiss that new lovers often use in the earliest, most tentative moments of their physical relationship.

"The Bent Kiss is what occurs when the heads of two lovers are bent toward each other, and when so bent, kissing takes place."

ONE OF THE most natural ways to kiss your lover is with your head angled slightly to one side, which permits maximum lip contact and deep tongue penetration. It's a superb means of expressing passion during foreplay and a great way to heighten excitement.

More Kissing

"When one of them turns up the face of the other by holding the head and chin, and then kissing, it is called a Turned Kiss."

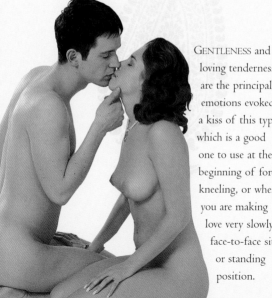

GENTLENESS and loving tenderness are the principal emotions evoked by a kiss of this type, which is a good one to use at the beginning of foreplay, kneeling, or when you are making love very slowly in a face-to-face sitting or standing position.

"After the Turned Kiss, try the Pressed Kiss, when the lower lip is pressed with much force. Another version, shown below, is the Greatly Pressed Kiss, in which one of the lovers holds the other's lower lip and then, after touching it with the tongue, kisses it with great force."

THESE ARE NOT REALLY KISSES, more an erotic prelude to kissing, in which the holding and forceful kissing of the lip represent an arousing variation on the theme.

Playing the Kissing Game

*T*he *Kama Sutra* describes a kissing game for lovers to play: "As regards kissing, a wager may be laid as to which will get hold of the lips of the other first. If the woman loses, she should pretend to cry, should keep her lover off by shaking her hands, and turn away from him and dispute with him saying, 'Let another wager be laid.'

If she loses this a second time, she should appear doubly distressed, and when her lover is off his guard or asleep, she should get hold of his lower lip, and hold it in her teeth, so that it should not slip away, and then she should laugh, make a loud noise, deride him, dance about, and say whatever she likes in a joking way, moving her eyebrows and rolling her eyes. The same may be applied to pressing, biting, and striking."

In his chapter on kissing, Vatsyayana describes three kinds of kisses that a young girl might give her partner. The places to be kissed are, he says, "the forehead, the eyes, the cheeks, the throat, the bosom, the breasts, the lips and the interior of the mouth." He describes the young girl's kisses as follows:

THE NOMINAL KISS
"When a girl only touches the mouth of her lover with her own ... it is called the nominal kiss."

THE THROBBING KISS
"When a girl wishes to touch the lip that is pressed into her mouth, and with that object moves her lower lip, but not the upper one, it is called the throbbing kiss."

THE TOUCHING KISS
"When a girl touches her lover's lip with her tongue, and having shut her eyes, places her hands on those of her lover, it is called the touching kiss."

Kissing the Body

"According to where on the body it is given, the intensity of a kiss should vary: it should be moderate, contracted, pressed, or soft."

ALTHOUGH THE LIPS and breasts are especially sensitive to the touch of the mouth, most parts of the body, including the limbs, respond to kissing; in general, the closer to the genitals the kiss is given, the more intense and irresistible the pleasure. There is no need for either partner to remain passive, because body kisses can be enjoyed by both partners at the same time.

Kissing and Licking

Caring lovers should pay special attention to sensitive areas like the breasts and the nipples, the insides of the thighs, and the backs of the knees. The greater your self-control in delaying penetration, the richer the rewards when it does occur.

Covering your partner's body systematically with kisses, or exploring it all over with your tongue (tongue bathing), is an excellent way to heighten anticipation.

WHEN KISSING THE BREASTS the most effective kisses are those that are applied lightly to the fullness of the breast, while the nipples may be sucked or nibbled gently. The nipples deserve special attention, because for many women, nipple stimulation is powerfully arousing.

The attentive lover devotes considerable time to kissing and fondling his partner's breasts, because for many women this produces a response that is as emotionally satisfying as it is physically exciting. Often, if her breasts are ignored in favor of her genitals, a woman feels cheated.

Biting

"Biting and teeth-marking of the breasts are described as 'The Broken Cloud' — biting which consists of unequal risings in a circle, and which comes from the space between the teeth."

MOST COUPLES WHO ENJOY giving love bites do not break the skin, preferring to suck their partner's flesh, often with the intention of leaving a mark as a token of possession. This type of ritual biting, intended to raise the skin between the teeth, not to pierce the skin, serves a similar purpose.

*❝The Biting of a Boar is the name given to a bite
for marking the shoulder. The bite consists of many broad
rows of marks near to one another, and with red intervals.
This is impressed on the breasts and the shoulders; and these
two last modes of biting are peculiar to
persons of intense passion.❞*

RESEARCH HAS REVEALED that women
are given to biting during lovemaking,
while many men feel somewhat
ambivalent about it and even more
so about being bitten. It has been
suggested, by way of explanation,
that because men are generally
more muscular than women, it
comes more naturally to
express their passion by
forceful bodily gestures
rather than through
biting.

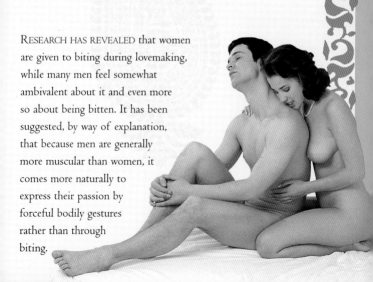

Cunnilingus

“The clitoris is probably the most sensitive part of a woman's body, and it responds best to gentle stimulation from the lips and tongue. Position yourself so that you can stroke your tongue upward over the shaft and head of her clitoris. Your partner can be standing, sitting, or lying on her back; if she is one of the many women who enjoy protracted cunnilingus and can experience a series of orgasms from it, she will usually be more comfortable lying down. Stimulate each side of the clitoris in turn, always from underneath. Use featherlight strokes on the head of the clitoris, and try flicking the underside of the shaft from side to side with the tip of your tongue.”

Stimulating the perineum is a great way to
enhance your lover's overall experience of
your lovemaking. When she opens her legs wide,
you can get between them to lick her perineum.
This is the area between the vagina and
the anus, and in most women it is rich in nerve
endings and so is very sensitive to being
touched, stroked, or licked. Stimulation of the
perineum can be highly arousing.

Oral Pleasure

"When you give your lover oral sex, a good way to create a slow but highly erotic crescendo of arousal is to kiss and lick her abdomen, her lower belly, and the insides of her thighs, slowly working in toward her genitals. Move on from this to kissing and licking her pubic mound, the outer lips of her vagina, and then her clitoris. A gradual approach such as this, perhaps even starting at her breasts and nipples and then working downward, helps build sexual tension, and is also useful if she is a little unsure about indulging in oral sex and needs a gentle introduction to genital kissing."

AFTER AROUSING YOUR LOVER by kissing and licking her clitoris and perineum, increase the stimulation by also darting your tongue in and out of her vagina. Start off by using just the tip of your tongue, then use the blade, and later alternate between shallow strokes with the tip and deep strokes with the blade.

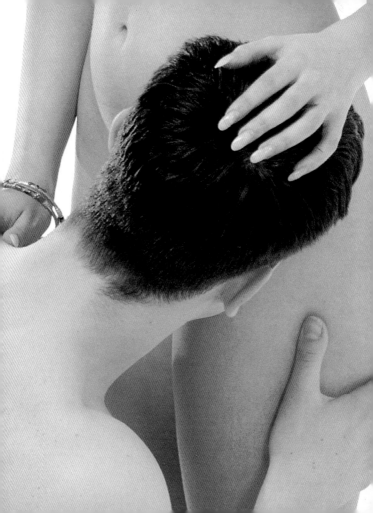

Fellatio

"Start your fellatio by licking his penis as though it were an ice cream cone. Hold its base in one hand and then, using the blade of your tongue, repeatedly lick upward, first on one side and then on the other. Try to vary the weight, length and intensity of your tongue strokes, in order to give your partner the greatest possible range of sensations and pleasure."

FLICKING YOUR TONGUE lightly along the ridge on the under side of his penis is a highly effective fellatio technique. At first, you may need to hold the base of his penis when you perform this move, but when you are adept at it, you will be able to perform it without using your hands, leaving them free to caress and fondle him.

Some women really adore the intimate pleasure of sucking their partner's penis, but are nervous about gagging during fellatio, particularly when he becomes excited and wants to thrust. You can overcome this fear by encircling the penis with one or both of your hands before kissing, licking, or sucking the end.

Congress of a Crow

" When a man and woman lie down in an inverted order, that is, with the head of one toward the feet of the other, and carry on this congress, it is called the congress of a crow. "

THIS TERSE ACCOUNT OF simultaneous oral sex in fact describes the classic "Sixty-Nine," in which the two partners perform simultaneous fellatio and cunnilingus. Whatever oral-genital stimulation lovers give each other individually, Sixty-Nine should allow them to do together. This may seem like an ideal arrangement that ensures truly mutual joy, but in reality it may prove awkward, and less satisfactory than practicing fellatio and cunnilingus in turn.

Kama Sutra
Positions

❖

LOVE POSITIONS

I n most people's minds, the words *Kama Sutra* evoke a beguiling blend of the exotic and the erotic, conjuring up visions of large numbers of impractical, bizarre, or even impossible lovemaking positions. We expect, when looking at a copy of this work, to see couples intertwined in dozens of different variations of sexual intercourse. Its name is synonymous with sexual variety. But, in fact, very little attention is paid to the act of intercourse alone. Vatsyayana lists only eight basic lovemaking positions. Most of these involve the woman lying on her back with her legs in a variety of different postures, but later in the *Kama Sutra*, Vatsyayana suggests three woman-on-top forms of lovemaking that should be used when a woman "acts the part of a man." He recommends that when a woman "sees that her lover is fatigued by constant congress, without having his desire satisfied, she should, with his permission, lay him down upon his back, and give him assistance by acting his part. She may also do this to satisfy the curiosity of her lover, or her own desire of novelty." Sound advice for all lovers, then and now.

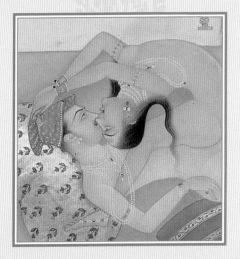

The Yawning Position

❝Lovemaking that begins with a straightforward man-on-top position, in which both partners' legs are outstretched, often develops naturally into the Yawning Position, in which the woman raises her thighs and parts them widely.❞

THE BARRIER PRESENTED by the woman's thighs in this position does not allow for very deep penetration, and it is unlikely that her clitoris will receive much stimulation. Offsetting this, though, is the undeniable eroticism of the position. Her genitals are displayed, and the helplessness she feels when in this position can be a powerful turn-on.

The Variant Yawning Position

“The deepest possible penetration is achieved with this variation on the Yawning Position. Because of the extreme depth of penetration, the woman should be fully aroused before her partner enters her.”

THIS IS THE POSITION you are most likely to slip into, with some relief, after playing with the Yawning Position. It is far more satisfactory, because it combines the ease of the missionary position with greater penetration and an erotic element derived from the woman's legs still being high in the air.

The Widely Opened Position

*"With her head thrown back, the woman arches her
back and raises her body to meet her partner,
opening her legs wide and giving an angle of entry
that ensures deep penetration."*

THE GENITAL CONTACT offered by this position is likely to bring more satisfaction to the woman than to the man. This is because it gives her clitoris full exposure to the friction of intercourse, but he may miss the feeling of tight containment he gets when she closes her legs against his penis.

The Position of the Wife of Indra

"Achievable only by the loosest of limb, this position is recommended as suitable for the 'highest congress' — love-making in which the vagina is fully open, ensuring maximum penetration. Most couples who try it, however, will probably use it simply as a brief interlude between less demanding postures. The position is named after Indrani, the beautiful and seductive wife of the Hindu deity Indra. He was the king of the gods in the early Vedic writings, and also the god of rain and thunder."

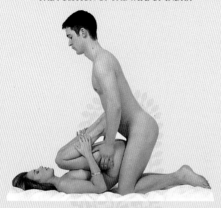

I THINK WE HAVE TO ASSUME that the Wife of Indra achieved a sense of deep sexual pleasure from being bundled up into a package. A woman can achieve considerable arousal by tensing her vaginal muscles, which happens when the legs are drawn up as close as possible to the body. In the buildup of sexual excitement, tension is vital. Orgasm is the relief of sexual tension, and without enough of it, it is very hard and sometimes impossible to achieve. The areas around the pelvis, in particular in the thighs and buttocks, fill with sexual engorgement, and it is possible to aid and enhance climax by deliberately building such excitement. Bioenergetic exercises, such as flexing the thighs and buttocks or practicing the Kegel exercises, can help in building up sexual arousal.

A Man's Duty to His Partner

Vatsyayana advises that a woman should marry a man "whom she thinks would be obedient to her, and capable of giving her pleasure." The *Kama Sutra* places the obligation on the man to satisfy his partner. To help him achieve this aim it offers a list of suggestions about how the man should move and perform during lovemaking.

MOVING FORWARD "when the organs are brought together properly and directly" – in other words, straightforward penetration.

CHURNING using your hand to hold and move the penis in the vagina.

PIERCING penetrating the vagina from above and pushing against "the upper part of the yoni" – the clitoris.

PRESSING rubbing and pressing the length of the shaft of the penis along the labia, but without actual penetration.

GIVING A BLOW penetration followed by withdrawal and striking the vagina with the penis.

BLOW OF THE BOAR rubbing one side of the vagina with the penis.

BLOW OF THE BULL rubbing both sides of the vagina with the penis.

SPORTING OF THE SPARROW rapid thrusting without withdrawal. Vatsyayana advises that "this takes place at the end of congress."

VIEW FROM THE 21ST CENTURY

The man's duty as described here is very penis-oriented by present-day standards. On the other hand Vatsyayana is quite right to take the emphasis off simple penetration, and focus more on stimulating the female genitals. We have almost forgotten that using the penis as a kind of vibrator can be immensely arousing. This is excellent advice.

A Woman's Duty to Her Partner

The *Kama Sutra* devotes several chapters to the correct conduct of women as wives, courtesans, and members of the royal harem. Duties ranging from housekeeping to herb gardening are detailed at length. Rather less is said about the woman's role during sexual intercourse. Only in the section, "When a woman acts the part of a man," does it get into specifics (acting the man's role involved "getting on top" – that is, sitting astride).

This reflects the *Kama Sutra's* overwhelmingly masculine bias – women are mostly portrayed as passive and submissive. Even the woman-on-top positions were seen as brief interludes in the normal progression of sex. Vatsyayana says that when the woman is tired she should "place her forehead on that of her lover, and should thus take rest." When she has had a chance to catch her breath, they should swap around – "normal service" is thus resumed. There is no instruction included for men, the somewhat "macho" assumption presumably being that men do not tire in the same way as women during lovemaking.

SEXUAL EQUALITY
Today we attribute greater sexual rights to the woman, and therefore also greater responsibility. Just as the man takes care to see that his partner is satisfied – if not through intercourse then through manual or oral sex – so too does the woman. If your partner stimulates you in a way you really enjoy, it's good to return the favor!

ADVICE TO WOMEN
If he doesn't take the initiative, why don't you? Don't let your partner do all the work, and don't be afraid to take the lead. As Vatsyayana says: "though a woman is reserved, and keeps her feelings concealed, yet when she gets on top of the man, she then shows all her love and desire."

Clasping Position

"This is more of an embrace than a practical position for sustained lovemaking, but the intertwining of limbs creates a feeling of special intimacy. In the man-on-top version of this position, the woman lies on her back and the man lies over her."

WESTERN LOVERS HAVE GENERALLY lost sight of the joys of foreplay and have focused instead on intercourse. Much of the pleasure to be obtained from good sex has thus been lost, and so there is more need today to use the clasping positions than we have had for centuries. The close, tender, and unhurried nature of these affectionate positions reminds us of what lovemaking is really all about; and it is easy to slip into more blatantly erotic ones when you are ready.

Side-by-Side Clasping Position

"For the gentle, relaxed, side-by-side version of the Clasping Position (see pages 94–95), the man should always lie on his left-hand side and the woman on her right."

SUCH A CLOSE, LOVING EMBRACE is highly reassuring for both partners, especially in the early days of a sexual relationship when lovemaking can sometimes be a cause for anxiety. Just the act of wrapping yourself lovingly around your partner and keeping it at that for a while can allay any anxieties, giving a comforting, unhurried start to making love with one another. An established couple will also find great pleasure and reassurance in adopting this position when they make love. Its gentle intimacy will allow them to reinforce their feelings of loving tenderness toward each other.

The Pressing Position

In fulfilling lovemaking, a sequence of positions often unfolds in which the lovers slip effortlessly from one embrace and one rhythm to another, like dancers. In this way, the Clasping Position leads naturally to the Pressing Position. Here, the woman grips her partner's thighs with her own to tighten her vagina around his thrusting penis.

WHAT IS WONDERFUL about spontaneous lovemaking is that it can flow like a beautiful dance where every inch of the body feels as if it is coming to life. Looked at in terms of arousal, that, of course, is exactly what happens. When the body reacts to intimate touch, the skin itself "erects," as tissues beneath it fill with fluid and muscle tension mounts. The more the partners roll around together and press their limbs against each other, the greater the sexual charge.

The Twining Position

"This variation of the Pressing Position (see pages 98–99) gives powerful expression to the woman's desire to weave herself about her partner. She places one leg across her lover's thigh and draws him to her."

AS THE CHOREOGRAPHY of the dance progresses, the breast tissues swell, the nipples erect, the muscles begin to tense, and the labia, clitoris, and penis become erect. As both partners become increasingly excited, their chests may display a sex flush — a patchy redness under the skin, beginning from below the rib cage and spreading up and across the breasts.

Creating Confidence in the Man

*I*n the *Kama Sutra*, the woman is encouraged to respond, if only in small ways, to her man. If he offers her a gift, it is helpful if she will take it. If he encourages her to talk, then it gives him something to go on if she is able to communicate with him. However, she is viewed as more desirable if she appears shy or reluctant to talk at first, but then responds.

THE WOMAN IS ENCOURAGED to give the man small gifts too, and to respond slowly but surely to his first kisses. Under some pretext or other she makes him look at special objects; narrates to him tales and stories very slowly. If she is seen casting sidelong glances as he moves away or is too affected by him to look him straight in the face, these are also viewed as a source of major encouragement.

ENCOURAGING YOUR MAN TODAY

These days almost the exact opposite is required of young women in order to inspire confidence in their suitor. Most research shows that men like to be approached, enjoy being asked out, and enjoy their woman taking the initiative in sex. However, having said that, they do not want to be dominated by their woman, and they do want sex to be mutually desired. They also prefer it when their women makes it abundantly clear that this is the case. In line with popular social mores and Hollywood tradition, there is some truth in the belief that woman who are slightly harder to get provoke more curiosity and therefore inspire more interest. But this does not work for all men and women. In the 21st century a kind of balance is valued. For a man to feel good, his woman needs to be straightforward yet not always available. She needs to offer him interested encouragement but appear to be deeply affected when he responds.

Creating Confidence in the Woman

For the first three days after marriage, the woman and her husband should sleep on the floor, abstain from sexual pleasures, and eat their food without seasoning.

FOR THE NEXT SEVEN DAYS they should bathe amid the sounds of auspicious musical instruments, should decorate themselves, dine together, and pay attention to their relations and to those who may have come to witness their marriage.

ON THE NIGHT OF THE TENTH DAY the man should begin in a lonely place with soft words and thus create confidence in the woman. Vatsyayana says that the man should begin to win her over, and create confidence in her, but should abstain at first from sexual pleasures.

HE SHOULD EMBRACE HER first of all in a way she likes most, because it does not last for a long time. If he is not well acquainted with her he should embrace her in darkness. This sound advice continues with the couple slowly getting comfortable with each other.

ON THE SECOND AND THIRD NIGHTS, he is then exhorted to feel her whole body with his hands and kiss her all over. He also shampoos her thighs, touches her private parts, loosens her dress but does not begin actual sex. Instead he talks, about himself, about her, and about the future.

THE VALUE OF STARTING SLOWLY

This slow start is a very practical way of creating trust in a partner and really not that different from how we try to do it today. If sex ever feels as if it is too fast, or trust has been damaged between partners, it is good advice to go back to some of these earlier stages. Modern sex therapy methods are based on something similar.

The Mare's Position

"This technique can be applied to enhance a number of positions. In it, the woman uses her vaginal muscles to squeeze the penis. This arouses pelvic sensuality for both him and her. Experimentation with different positions will reveal which one the vaginal squeeze works with effectively. For many people, the best is the man-on-top Clasping Position, but others find it enjoyable where the woman sits astride the man, either facing him or with her back to him."

THIS TECHNIQUE SHOWS that there is nothing new under the sun. Since about the 1970s, we in the West have been teaching young women to exercise and use their PC (pubococcygeal) muscles through the use of Kegel exercises. This helps them improve their vaginal tone after having babies, to improve their orgasmic response (stronger vaginal muscles will lead to more powerful orgasms), and to give their male partners extra stimulation.

The Rising Position

"The woman raises her legs straight up, above the shoulders of the man, who kneels in front of her and puts his penis into her vagina. By pressing her thighs together, she squeezes him and increases the friction as he moves, producing exquisite sensations for both."

SINCE HIS PARTNER'S calves and feet are in easy reach of his hands, the man can either caress them or hold them to steady himself during vigorous thrusting and she can caress his thighs at the same time.

The Half-Pressed Position

"From the Rising Position, the woman stretches one leg straight out, past her partner's side, and bends her other leg at the knee, placing the sole of her foot on his chest. Because this position constricts the vagina, the man should take care not to thrust too hard; otherwise, the woman will feel discomfort rather than intense pleasure."

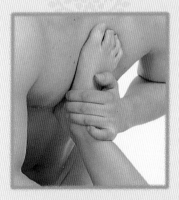

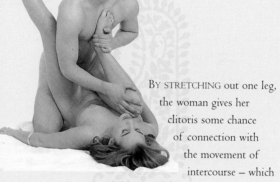

BY STRETCHING out one leg, the woman gives her clitoris some chance of connection with the movement of intercourse – which she cannot do in the Pressed Position because her clitoris is tucked away between her thighs. Stretching is in itself a sexy sensation, and this may encourage the woman to move carefully under her man so that the shaft of the penis gets some extra vaginal vibration. Having one of the woman's feet flat on his chest is likely to increase the intensity of the man's feelings, just as it does when, at other times, she tenderly places her hand or head there. It can be a surprisingly loving gesture should he choose to caress her foot, possibly even raising it to kiss as a demonstration of affection.

The Pressed Position

“Instead of putting only one of her feet on the man's chest, as in the Half-Pressed Position, the woman draws her thighs back to her chest, bends her legs at the knee, and places the soles of both her feet against his chest. The sensations for both partners will be subtly different from those produced by the Half-Pressed Position, but the man must find a depth and force of penetration that avoids causing pain to her shortened vagina.”

THIS POSITION, like the Half-Pressed, is one in which the woman assumes a submissive posture. When the man presses his partner's feet with his hand, the woman feels even more vulnerable and the man more powerful.

The Splitting of a Bamboo

❝This aptly named position calls for a simple evolution from the basic man-on-top posture, which requires considerable suppleness in the woman. She raises one leg and puts it on her partner's shoulder for a while, then brings that leg down and raises the other. This sequence can be repeated over and over again.❞

POSITIONS SUCH as this remind me of the way young couples use their bodies and have fun inventing crazy sex positions during the early days of their physical relationship.

Fixing of a Nail

"Instead of putting her leg on her partner's shoulder, as in the Splitting of a Bamboo, the woman places her heel on his forehead. Her leg and foot then resemble a hammer driving in a nail, represented by his head."

HAVE FUN WHILE MAKING LOVE — no one has decreed that sex should be a solemn business. Positions such as this are meant to be enjoyed in a lighthearted manner.

The Lotus-like Position

"Imitating the lotus yoga position, the woman draws in her legs, folding one over the other as neatly as possible, so that the vagina is pulled up to meet the penis."

MOST WOMEN WHO TRY this challenging position find that they cannot hold it for long, if indeed at all. Sadly not all of us possess the suppleness of a gymnast!

The Crab's Position

"In this picturesque and graphic love position, the woman bends and draws in both legs and rests her thighs on her stomach, rather like a crab retracting its claws. The man thrusts in close from a kneeling position."

PLAY IS AN IMPORTANT part of the early stages of any relationship, and play in sex is no exception. When indulging in playful behavior, for instance by adopting positions such as this, we subconsciously learn a lot about each other.

Turning Position

"When lovemaking in the basic man-on-top position, the man can, with practice, lift one leg and turn around without withdrawing from her, so that he eventually lies in the opposite direction."

DURING LOVEMAKING, varying a
position can often be used to
increase the feeling of intimacy.
In this case, while the man turns
around, his partner can demonstrate
tenderness toward him by
embracing or caressing his back,
shoulders, and sides.

Turning Position Stage-by-Stage

FIRST STAGE The first stage in the series of moves that make up the Turning Position is to begin your lovemaking in the man-on-top ("missionary") position. The man should lie with both legs between those of his partner.

SECOND STAGE
The man lifts
first his left leg
and then his right
leg over her right
leg, without
withdrawing.

THIRD STAGE He
supports himself
on his arms and
moves both legs
around, again
without
withdrawing.

FOURTH STAGE In
this final stage, he
ends up with his
body between her
legs and one leg
on either side of
her shoulders.

The Suspended Congress

"As the man leans against a wall, the woman puts her arms around his neck, while he lifts her by holding her thighs or by locking his hands beneath her bottom. She grips his waist with her thighs and pushes her feet against the wall."

THIS IS A POSITION that calls for a fair amount of strength in the man. If the woman is light, however, he may be able to support her with one arm around her waist, using the other hand to caress her.

The Supported Congress

The support referred to in this position is gained by leaning against a wall or by one partner bracing the weight of the other.

SOMETIMES, WHEN SUDDEN passion overwhelms, a couple may prefer to dispense with the preliminaries and make love standing up. The advantage of leaning against a wall is that, with the woman firmly supported, the man finds it easier to thrust vigorously.

The Top

"This movement requires considerable dexterity and is achieved through practice. While sitting astride her partner, the woman raises her legs to clear his body and swivels around on his penis. While she is perfecting this maneuver, the woman should take care not to lose her balance; otherwise, she may hurt both herself and her partner."

THIS POSITION and its variant, the Swing, although just about possible, really have to be the ancient Indians' idea of a joke. Most of the damage the moves could cause would be suffered by the male partner. In the case of the Top, he could end up with an injured penis. Not a position to be encouraged.

The Swing

"In this variation on the Top, the man should lie with his back arched. However, this is only feasible if the man has a strong back, and even then it is unlikely that he could sustain the posture for very long. It is more practical for him either to lie flat, as here, or to prop himself up on his arms."

THE GREAT THING about the Swing, at least from the man's point of view, is that she has to do all the work while he enjoys himself. However, the position is good for the woman, in that she has great control and may enjoy a sense of power.

The Pair of Tongs

"With her legs bent at the knee, the woman sits astride, facing the man, who lies flat on his back. She draws his penis inside her and squeezes it repeatedly with her vagina, holding it for a long time. Penetration is deep."

THIS POSITION IS PERHAPS the most practical of the three woman-on-top positions. By using her vaginal muscles, the woman may stimulate her man while also arousing herself. Some women use vaginal fluttering to give pleasure, and combining this with a little movement can be a gentle method of sexual enjoyment.

The Elephant Posture

"The woman lies with her breasts, stomach, thighs, and feet all touching the bed, and the man lies over her with the small of his back arched inward. Once he is inside her, the woman can intensify the sensations for both partners by pressing her thighs closely together."

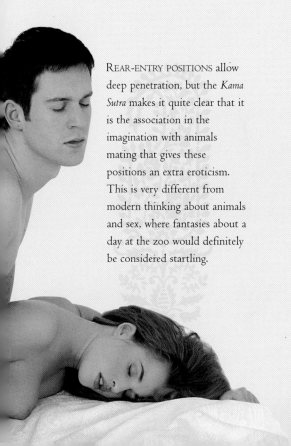

REAR-ENTRY POSITIONS allow deep penetration, but the *Kama Sutra* makes it quite clear that it is the association in the imagination with animals mating that gives these positions an extra eroticism. This is very different from modern thinking about animals and sex, where fantasies about a day at the zoo would definitely be considered startling.

The Congress of a Cow

❝The powerful symbolism of mating animals can serve to heighten passion for many couples. In this challenging variation on the more common rear-entry postures in which the woman kneels, she supports herself on her hands and feet and her partner mounts her like a bull. It makes deep penetration possible and allows the man to control the depth and power of his thrusts.**❞**

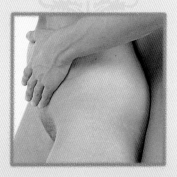

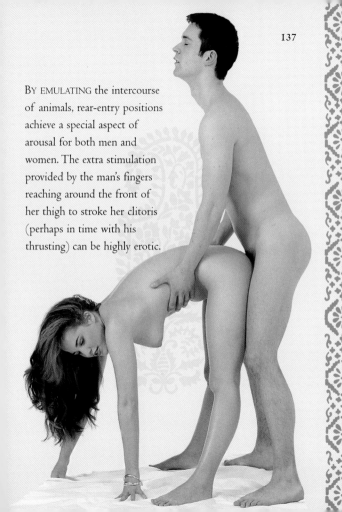

BY EMULATING the intercourse of animals, rear-entry positions achieve a special aspect of arousal for both men and women. The extra stimulation provided by the man's fingers reaching around the front of her thigh to stroke her clitoris (perhaps in time with his thrusting) can be highly erotic.

The Power of the Imagination

*E*ven in modern times the subject of sexual fantasies has only lately shaken off its taboo status. As early as the 4th century, however, the *Kama Sutra* appreciated the role of fantasy, understanding that it enhances the pleasures of lovemaking and keeps sex fresh and varied. In the original text, it suggests that, by seeking inspiration from the mating habits of the animal kingdom, imaginative lovers can greatly extend their repertoires.

After describing the congress of a cow, where the lovers harness the erotically charged symbolism of the potent bull, the *Kama Sutra* recommends imitating different kinds of "congress." There's the congress of a dog, the congress of a goat, the congress of a deer, the forcible mounting of an ass (!), the congress of a cat, the jump of a tiger, the pressing of an elephant, the rubbing of a boar, and the mounting of a horse. And in all these cases the characteristics of the different animals should be manifested by acting like them." Despite appearances, Vatsyayana did not intend the *Kama Sutra* to be a handbook of bestiality. What he is driving at here is that by using the imagination it is possible to keep sex constantly fresh and exciting. One of the most common causes for declining sexual desire over the course of a long relationship is boredom. The key to overcoming sexual boredom is variety, fueled by the power of fantasy and ceaselessly imaginative experimentation.

LETTING YOURSELF GO

Sexual fantasy offers extra erotic stimulation to women who find it difficult or impossible to climax or let go of their inhibitions and self-consciousness. By sharing fantasies, lovers open up to one another, deepening their sense of intimacy and enhancing their emotional connections.

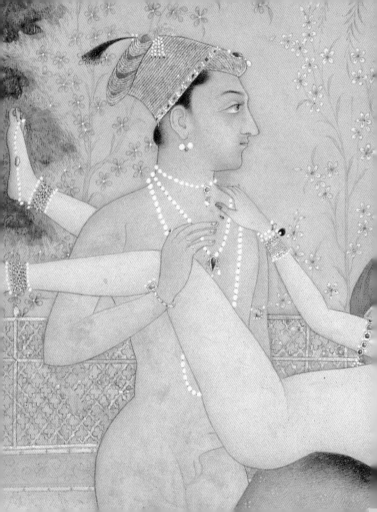

Ananga
Ranga
Positions

ANANGA RANGA POSITIONS

The *Ananga Ranga* shares common origins with the *Kama Sutra*, but was written up to 1,500 years later, probably in the late 15th or early 16th century. It was translated into Arabic and, as a result, it exerted a strong influence on the sexual attitudes of the Islamic world. The late-medieval India of the *Ananga Ranga* was, like the Arab world, much more ordered than that which produced the *Kama Sutra*. Sexuality was freely expressed within and outside marriage in the time of Vatsyayana, but Kalyana Malla, the author of the *Ananga Ranga*, reflected a rigid society that censured extramarital sex. The major practical difference between the two Indian classics is that the *Kama Sutra* was written for lovers, married or otherwise, while the *Ananga Ranga* does not question the sanctity of marriage and explicitly offers instruction to the married man. Equally clear is the author's motive for writing the *Ananga Ranga* in the first place — to protect marriage from the sexual tedium that, then as now, can so easily set in. It also offers an edge to lovemaking not previously mentioned, which is that of the spiritual. Kama's Wheel is about sexual contemplation.

Level Feet Posture

❝In this position, the man lifts his partner's body, bracing himself against her, and places her outstretched legs over his shoulders. If the partners are just the right size, she can rest her buttocks on the bed but, although this is not as demanding, it is less mutually stimulating.❞

COUPLES WHO LIKE deep penetration find that this position is a good one. The man gets a sense of control because he can move her into the most comfortable shape to suit his need to penetrate, while she acquires a sense of helplessness that can be powerfully erotic.

Raised Feet Posture

"In this position, lying on her back, the woman bends her legs at the knees and draws them back. Her partner then enters her from the kneeling position."

BECAUSE THE MAN IS kneeling, he does not need to use his hands to support himself or to maintain his balance, so he can comfortably use his hands to caress his partner and fondle her breasts. And by raising her hips with both hands, he can penetrate her at an angle that allows his penis to stimulate the front wall of her vagina, along which is located the highly sensitive G-spot.

The Refined Posture

"Instead of resting on her partner's shoulders, as in the Level Feet Posture, the woman's legs pass on either side of his waist. This allows deep penetration, and greater stimulation is possible if the man raises the woman by using his hands to support her buttocks."

WHEN HE IS LIFTING her and supporting her buttocks, he can apply a little gentle pressure to draw the buttocks away from the anus and perineum. This will provide her with extra erotic sensation.

Kama's Wheel

"The man sits with his legs outstretched and parted, and his partner lowers herself onto his penis, extending her legs over his. He then passes his arms on either side of her body, keeping them straight. In this way he completes the spoke-like pattern of limbs that gives the position its name."

KAMA'S WHEEL ILLUSTRATES a dimension of sexuality that most of us probably find hard to comprehend. It's a dimension that allows sex, like a type of meditation, to bring us a high level of awareness and increased sense of well-being. The object of the Kama's Wheel is not to build erotic feeling, or to achieve orgasm. It is rather to obtain a balance of mind that feels clear, calm, and happy. If you are interested in using sexual energies to investigate new mental experiences, the Kama's Wheel is worth trying.

The Intact Posture

"While lying on her back, the woman raises her legs and bends them at the knee, so that they rest against her partner's chest when he kneels between her thighs. Before entering her, he puts his hands below her buttocks and lifts her up slightly."

THE INTACT POSTURE IS another lovemaking position where the woman is treated like a package and the man makes the moves. If control and helplessness are important aspects of your relationship, then this could be extremely arousing mentally, although in sexual terms it is not particularly satisfactory for the woman.

The Placid Embrace

*In this position, the woman lies on
her back and the man, kneeling, lifts
her buttocks and enters her. By crossing
her ankles behind his back, she can draw
him closer to her and increase the
feeling of intimacy.*

THE MAIN feeling
associated with this
move is that of great
tenderness. It involves a
pure embrace, in that she
twines both her arms and
her legs around her lover
as an expression
of love and
trust in him.

The Gaping Position

"In the Gaping Position, pillows or cushions are used to arch the woman's body. The opening of the vagina receives strong stimulation, and for this reason some women value the position as a prelude to deeper penetration."

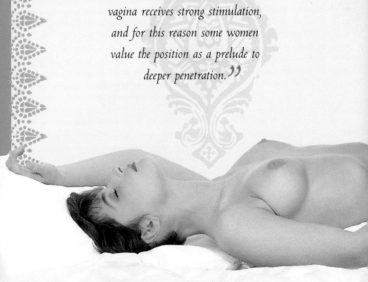

RAISING THE PELVIS WITH cushions, so that the genitals are more open than they are when she is lying flat, was a favorite sex therapy technique in the 1950s for women who didn't reach orgasm. The theory behind this technique is that if the clitoris is exposed to the thrust of intercourse, it is more likely to be stimulated. However, stimulation is usually achieved more efficiently by nimble fingerwork.

The Encircling Position

The Encircling Position is very well fitted for those burning with desire. While lying on her back, the woman raises her feet off the bed a little and crosses her calves so that her legs form a diamond shape. Then the man lies over her and enters her.

FOR HER, THERE ARE shades of bondage attached to this position, which, combined with the fact that her pelvis is opened wide and her clitoris is exposed, gives a very sensual approach to intercourse. Penetration is not particularly deep, but her very openness is an intriguing idea for her lover.

The Splitting Position

"Here, the woman lies on her back and her partner
enters her from the kneeling position.
He then lifts her legs straight up, resting
them on his shoulder."

POSITIONS SUCH AS THIS are
excellent for the older man
who needs a more robust
sensation during intercourse.
His penis is snugly
contained by her vagina, and
the extra gripping sensation of
her thighs gives the additional
friction that he needs to
bring him to orgasm.

The Crab Embrace

"In this warm and inviting variation on the basic side-by-side position, the man enters the woman and lies between her thighs. One of her legs remains beneath his, and she passes the other over his body, just below his chest."

PENETRATION IS DEEP in this position, but the man's movements may be restricted. Like all the side-by-side positions, it is useful when either partner is tired but still passionate. When describing a side-by-side position, the *Kama Sutra* says that the man should lie on his left side and the woman on her right. This rule is not mentioned by Kalyana Malla, but the suggestion was no doubt prompted by the fact that, then as now, most men were right-handed. However, if the man is left-handed and wants to caress his partner with that hand, or if the woman wants to caress her partner with her right hand, it makes sense to reverse the position.

The Transverse Lute

"The lovers lie side by side with their legs outstretched. After the woman has raised one leg slightly to allow her partner to enter her, he raises one leg and rests it on her thigh."

SIDE-BY-SIDE POSITIONS are excellent for men who need more friction during intercourse. The penis thrusts are felt along the insides of the labia, which are pressed against the penis by the legs, so these positions also give the woman an increased likelihood of orgasm. And if the man pulls himself up a little higher in relation to the woman (that is, toward her head), he can ensure that his penis brushes against her clitoris. These positions are often used as part of sex therapy for women who have had difficulty achieving orgasms.

The Four Orders of Women

The authors of both the *Ananga Ranga* and the *Kama Sutra* were fond of lists and categories. The *Ananga Ranga* classifies women according to their temperament into four Orders, each of which details a variety of female characteristics. These orders correspond loosely to the modern body types but are pretty fanciful, and none too flattering if you fall into the wrong end of the spectrum!

THE PADMINI, OR LOTUS-WOMAN

Her face is as pleasing as the full moon; her body, well clothed with flesh, is soft as the *Shiras* (a tall fragrant tree) or mustard flower; her skin is fine, tender and fair as the yellow lotus. Her *yoni* (vagina) resembles the opening lotus-bud, and her *kama-salila* (vaginal secretion) is perfumed like the lily.

THE CHITRINI, OR ART-WOMAN

She is of middle size, neither short nor tall, with jet-black hair, thin, round, shell-like neck; tender body; waist lean-girthed as the lion's; hard, full breasts — and heavily made hips. The hair is thin around the yoni, the Mons Veneris being soft, raised and round. The kama-salila is hot, and has the perfume of honey. Her eyes roll and her walk is coquettish.

THE SHANKHINI, OR CONCH-WOMAN

She is of bilious temperament, her skin being always hot and tawny, or dark yellow-brown; her body is large and heavy, her waist thick and her breasts small. Her yoni is ever moist with kama-salila, which is distinctly salt, and the cleft is covered with thick hair.

THE HASTINI, OR ELEPHANT-WOMAN

She is short of stature; she has a coarse, stout body, and her skin, if fair, is of dead white. Her kama-salila has the savor of juice that flows in spring from the elephant's temples.

The Three Orders of Men

*T*he *Ananga Ranga*'s classification of men follows that of the *Kama Sutra*. Men are divided into three Orders: the hare man, bull man, and horse man. As with the women, Vatsyayana keeps his classification genital – in this case it depends on the dimensions of the man's *lingam* (penis). Kalyana Malla, author of the *Ananga Ranga*, extrapolates from this to give a precise description of each type. The descriptions are not exactly flattering in terms of modern sensibilities – and particularly if you happen to fall into the wrong category!

THE SHASHA (HARE MAN)

The Shasha is known by a lingam that in erection does not exceed six finger-breadths, or about three inches (7.5 cm). His figure is short and spare but well proportioned in shape and make; he has small hands, feet, knees, loins and thighs.

His features are clear and well proportioned. He is humble in demeanor; his appetite for food is small, and he is moderate in his carnal desires. Finally, there is nothing offensive in his semen.

THE VRISHABHA (BULL MAN)

The Vrishabha is known by a lingam of nine fingers in length or four inches and a half (11.4 cm). His body is robust and tough, like that of a tortoise. His disposition is cruel and violent, restless and irascible, and his semen is ever-ready.

THE ASHWA (HORSE MAN)

The Ashwa is known by a lingam of twelve fingers, or about six inches (15 cm) long. He is tall and large-framed, but not fleshy, and his delight is in big and robust women, never in those of delicate form. He is reckless in spirit, passionate and covetous, gluttonous, volatile, lazy, and full of sleep. He cares little for the venereal rite, except when the spasm approaches. His semen is copious, salt and goatlike.

The Lotus Position

"In this most straightforward of sitting positions the man sits cross-legged and the woman sits on his lap, facing him, and lowers herself onto his penis. The man may place his hands on his partner's shoulders, but he can just as comfortably, and perhaps more affectionately, put his arms around her body or about her neck."

THE SITTING POSITIONS CAN be friendly, charged with eroticism, youthful, comic, acrobatic, or fun, depending on your frame of mind. They are mainly positions with which to give the male a treat, for it is the woman who tends to do all the work. One of the great strengths of the Indian love texts, however, is that although they always appear to be written from a male point of view, they are very fair, given their era, in paying attention to the sexual needs of both partners.

The Accomplishing Position

"This variation on the Lotus Position requires the woman to raise one leg slightly, perhaps using her hand to help keep her balance. Having one leg raised changes the tension between her vagina and his penis."

LIKE THE OTHER face-to-face positions, this one allows the couple to kiss and the man to fondle the woman's breasts. However, the man's thrusting movements are restricted.

The Position of Equals

"Sitting astride the man and facing him, the woman stretches out her legs alongside his body, passing them under his arms at about elbow height."

ACCORDING TO KALYANA MALLA, the man should lift the woman's legs into position when she is seated astride his lap, but in the heat of passion either partner may make the adjustment from the straightforward sitting posture out of which this usually develops. It is further suggested that he should clasp his hands about her neck, but the position is one in which the hands might play a more active role, and it is worth taking advantage of this fact.

Sexual Tension and Multiple Orgasms

The position of the Wife of Indra (see pages 88–89) demonstrates that some of the ancient positions were designed with the aim of increasing sexual tension. By building up the degree of tension in the vaginal muscles and surrounding parts of the body, a woman can experience a more intense orgasm when that tension is explosively relieved. Similar principles apply for couples where the woman is capable of experiencing multiple orgasm.

THE VARIOUS SITTING POSITIONS suggested by the *Ananga Ranga* assist these activities. Since they do not allow for any vigorous thrusting they are not too tiring, and they allow couples more control over the buildup of sexual tension than is possible with many other positions. On the other hand, they can make it difficult for the man to sustain the delicate balance between getting sufficient stimulation and losing his erection. Use manual and oral stimulation to help the man regain his erection without allowing erotic tension to flag for either partner.

BUILD UP YOUR SEXUAL TENSION

The American sex researchers Hartman and Fithian recommend that such a couple takes intercourse slowly. They should not go in for a great deal of vigorous thrusting, but let their desire and response develop gradually. This is because in order to enjoy multiple orgasms they need a far greater buildup of sexual tension than they do for a single climax. Time is needed to tease and tantalize the senses, so it is unwise to wear yourself out by treating your lovemaking as a gymnastics session. To sustain a bout of sex long enough to reach the point of multiple orgasm involves overcoming three main obstacles: both partners need to avoid climaxing too soon; the man needs to be able to keep his erection, despite continually pulling back from the brink; and they both need to sustain their energy levels for long enough.

The Snake Trap

In this position, the woman sits astride the man, facing him, and each partner holds the other's feet. This arrangement allows the couple to rock themselves back and forth in a stimulating seesaw-like movement but, since it restricts thrusting, it is best adopted when the man is tired, or is satisfied and is making love again for his partner's pleasure.

THIS POSITION IS AN example of sexual play. There is no way in which it serves any real purpose with regard to sexual stimulation, but it can be delightful for just "fooling around." It could also be used in a slow buildup to more energetic sexual activity, and it provides just enough stimulation to keep sexual interest going.

The Paired Feet Position

"The man sits with his legs wide apart while the woman lowers herself onto him, with her legs over his. During full penetration, he presses her thighs together."

NEITHER PARTNER CAN MOVE very much in this position, but the pressure of the woman's thighs constricts her vagina, producing pleasurable sensations for both the man and woman alike.

The Crying Out Position

"The man lifts the woman by passing her legs over his arms at the elbow, and moves her from side to side. In a variation known as the Monkey Position, the man moves the woman backward and forward rather than from side to side."

BECAUSE THE MAN has to lift the woman and move her around on his penis, this position is best, perhaps only, suited to a strong man and a light woman.

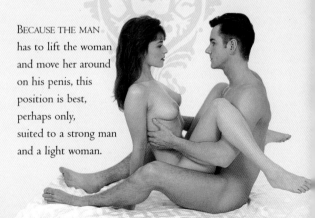

The Orgasmic Role-Reversal

"Kalyana Malla likens the woman's posture in this position to that of a 'large bee' and asserts that she 'thoroughly satisfies herself.' She squats on the man's thighs, then inserts his penis, closes her legs firmly, and adopts a churning motion."

BECAUSE OF THE FREEDOM of movement that this position gives to the woman, she can control the speed, angle, and amount by which she moves her pelvis in circles and from side to side. She can also add extra variety to the sensations she feels by varying the depth of penetration.

The Ascending Position

For the woman whose 'passion has not been gratified by previous copulation,' the Ascending Position is recommended. Sitting cross-legged on the man's thighs, she should 'seize' his penis and insert it into her vagina.

As in similar positions, the woman can alter the angle of her partner's penis to give herself the kind of stimulation she wants; in particular, she can ensure that the G-spot receives attention. She can also stimulate her clitoris.

The Inverted Embrace

"The man lies on his back. The woman lies on top of him and inserts his penis. Pressing her breast to his and steadying herself by gripping his waist, she moves her hips in every direction."

LIKE THE OTHER woman-on-top position shown here, the Inverted Embrace puts her in control of the movements of lovemaking. The feeling of power that this gives can increase her excitement – just as the man's pleasure can be increased if he is not afraid of relinquishing control.

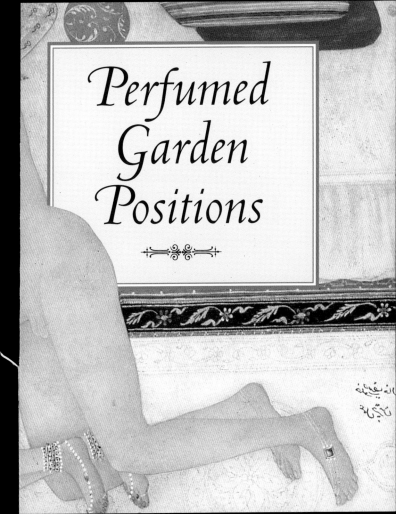

Perfumed Garden Positions

الله يفينه
ثأدبرله

PERFUMED LOVE

I n the male-dominated North African culture of the late 15th century in which it was written, Sheikh Nefzawi's *The Perfumed Garden* would have been regarded as something to be hidden away from the women-folk, a manual of practical advice with which they had no need to concern themselves. It provided ample instruction on what a man could do to, and with, his wife or mistress, but barely touched on her experience. Even though its outlook feels dated, and perhaps even alien, *The Perfumed Garden* goes to the heart of the matter, explaining a wealth of positions and techniques that will, in fact, deepen the experience of lovemaking for man and woman alike. As more and more women are freeing themselves from the sexual stereotyping that has traditionally turned them into mere objects of men's desire, many are actively seeking ways in which to increase their own sexual pleasure. For them, the primary goal is to cast off the passive role and feel free to decide with their partners what they want from sex. Exploring the positions on the following pages should form part of that quest.

First Posture

" A straightforward man-on-top position, the First Posture is particularly suitable for the man with a long penis, allowing him to control the depth to which he penetrates his lover. "

IN THE PERFUMED GARDEN, Sheikh Nefzawi makes sensible allowances for physical differences between men and women. Here, for example, is a classic position in which a man with a long penis could easily adjust his length of thrust so as not to hurt his partner. This is a very real consideration when partners are of greatly differing builds.

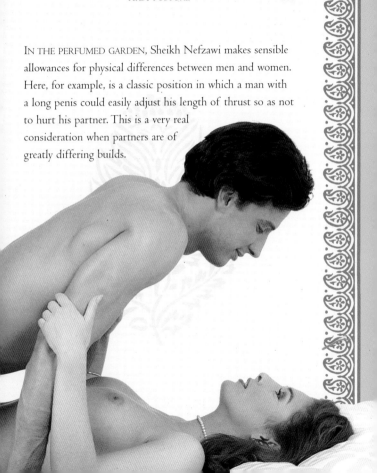

Second Posture

"This can hardly be described as a comfortable position for the woman, but it is recommended to the man who has only a short penis."

A SHORT PENIS is something that many men feel ashamed of, and fortunes are made by companies that claim to be able to extend or enlarge the smaller man. The second posture is a very practical method of making intercourse possible for the man who is particularly underendowed, but I suspect that most women would find it too difficult or uncomfortable. In that event, the couple should consider alternatives to intercourse that will give satisfaction to both partners. These include masturbation, mutual masturbation, oral sex, and the use of sex aids.

Third Posture

"This is an excellent posture to use when you want really deep penetration, and is similar to the Yawning Position of the Kama Sutra."

ALTHOUGH THIS POSTURE ALLOWS the maximum possible penetration, I recommend that it be attempted only when the woman is fully aroused, to ensure that her vagina is ready to be penetrated deeply. During sexual arousal, the vaginal canal undergoes a process called tenting, which involves the enlargement of its upper end to accommodate the deep-thrusting penis.

Fourth Posture

"Varying the angle at which the man enters his partner can create a novel range of sensations for both of them. The Fourth Posture, in which the man places both his partner's legs over his shoulders before he enters her, enables the couple to find the most pleasurable angles of entry."

AN IGNORANT LOVER can unwittingly hurt both himself and his partner if he attempts to enter her at the wrong angle, but by raising her body a little before penetration he is unlikely to do harm. It is, of course, a good idea for him to have kissed, cuddled, fondled, and stroked her long before they begin sexual intercourse, so that she is properly aroused and her vaginal juices have begun to flow.

Fifth Posture

“In this, the simplest side-by-side position, both partners lie with legs outstretched, and the woman raises her uppermost leg to allow the man to enter her.”

LOVEMAKING POSITIONS in which the
man and woman lie side by side and
facing each other, as they do in this one,
are excellent for inspiring deep feelings of
loving tenderness. Positions such as this
one facilitate close eye contact, kissing
and nuzzling, all of which enhance the
loving feelings that are part of good sex.

Movements of Love

THE BUCKET IN THE WELL
"The man and the woman join in close embrace after the introduction. Then he gives a push and withdraws a little; the woman follows him with a push, and also retires. So they continue their alternative movement, keeping proper time. Placing foot against foot, and hand against hand, they keep up the motion of a bucket in a well."

THE MUTUAL SHOCK
"After the introduction they each draw back, but without dislodging the member completely. Then they both push tightly together and thus go on keeping time."

THE APPROACH
"The man moves as usual and then stops. Then the woman, with the member in her receptacle, begins to move like the man and then stops."

Love's Tailor

"The man, with his member being only partially inserted, keeps up a sort of quick friction with the part that is in, and then suddenly plunges his member in up to its root."

The Toothpick in the Vulva

"The man introduces his member between the walls of the vulva, and then drives it right up and down, and right and left. Only a man with a vigorous member can do this."

The Boxing-Up of Love

"The man introduces his member entirely into the vagina, so closely that his hairs are mixed up with the woman's. He must now move forcibly, without withdrawing his tool in the least."

Remember to take care at all times not to hurt your partner – vaginas and penises are sensitive organs, and can be easily bruised or damaged. Start slowly, and take special care with movements like the "Toothpick."

Sixth Posture

"Because he enters the woman from a kneeling position, the man has his hands free to caress her back and breasts and stimulate her clitoris. Alternatively, he can hold her waist and pull her back and forth on his member."

I THINK THIS CLASSIC rear-entry posture generates a powerful, primal eroticism. If at some time in our evolution we were truly apelike, we would have copulated in this style. The buttocks are considered by anthropologists to give out strong sexual signals, and it has been suggested that the only reason the breasts in the human female are as fully developed as they are, compared to those of other primates, is because they are imitating the visual appeal of the buttocks.

Seventh Posture

> *In this posture, the woman should be lying on her side while the man kneels and lifts one of her legs onto his shoulder, but it is marginally less difficult if she lies on her back.*

WHETHER THE WOMAN LIES on her side or on her back, this position is for acrobats and not to be taken seriously. You might, however, have a lot of fun incorporating it into a circus fantasy.

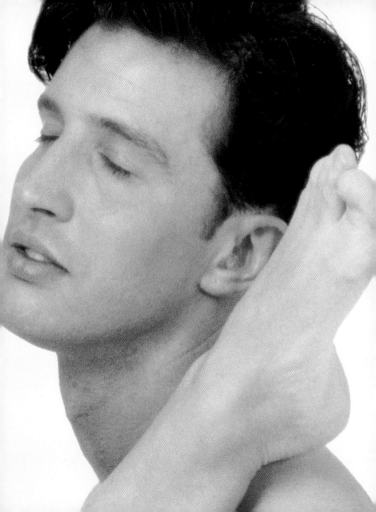

Eighth Posture

By changing the position of the woman's hips, the man can vary the angle and depth of penetration, and because he is kneeling, his hands are free to caress her body. She can either pull her crossed legs back before he enters her, or cross her legs beneath her thighs so he can kneel astride her.

Each of the two variations on this cross-legged posture has its own special advantages. I suggest that you use the legs-pulled-back version when you wish for deep penetration and G-spot stimulation, and the legs-under-the-thighs version for clitoral stimulation.

Ninth Posture

This highly erotic posture can provide quite a variety of sensations because it has three main variants — two rear-entry and one face-to-face — and is one that lends itself to making love when clothed as well as when naked.

In the rear-entry versions, the woman can either lie facedown across a bed with her knees on the floor, or stand and lean forward over it. In the face-to-face version, she lies on her back on a bed with her feet on the floor.

TODAY, THIS IS the
position that is featured most often
in fantasies (and in the reality) of
making love on the kitchen table,
on an office desk, or on some other
unconventional surface.

Tenth Posture

"Despite appearances, this is a position that puts the woman in charge — movement for both partners is limited, but she initiates it and he must respond to her rhythms. The woman lies on the bed with her legs stretched out and parted, and he kneels between her thighs. When he has inserted his member, the man bends forward and grips the headboard, and the lovers move back and forth with a seesaw motion."

PULLING AND pushing against the bed in this manner can improve the sensation of lovemaking so that it feels more decisive and exciting.

Eleventh Posture

“Although the woman's movements in response to her partner's are limited in this position, they are likely to be compensated for by the intense stimulation it provides and the depth of penetration that can be achieved.”

THIS CLASSIC POSITION allows deep
penetration and good clitoral stimulation.
The movement of intercourse will pull the
woman's labia rhythmically across her
clitoris, creating a gentle, stimulating
friction that may trigger orgasm.

Before
and After
Love

GETTING CLOSE TO YOUR PARTNER

M odern and ancient forms of sex therapy agree that scaling the heights of sexual ecstasy depends on more than the purely physical aspects of sex. Tantric sex focuses as much on building a spiritual bond between lovers as on the act. Modern therapeutic programs echo this by working on intimacy and empathy between partners before moving on to sex. Getting closer to your partner is particularly important in programs aimed at rekindling flagging desire. Such programs emphasize building up tactile pleasure without, at first, any sexual imperative, so that sensuality becomes a strong bond once more between the lovers, and a sound basis upon which to build desire.

Over the following pages I outline a three-day program, based on a Tantric model, which comes with a strict rule about sexual continence: there will be no intercourse or orgasm until the latter part of the third day. Do your best not to give way to longings that lead to coupling – some of the practices can be deeply arousing. There is a purpose for this proscription against intercourse – the Tantric ideal is to prolong the entire sex act so that it becomes greatly enhanced.

Time for Intimacy

*M*any couples complain that finding the time and space to be intimate with one another is a major hurdle in maintaining loving sex. Between kids and jobs there is often little of either left over. Making some time for yourself and each other – whether it involves simply putting a lock on your bedroom door or packing the kids off to grandparents – is a vital step toward reclaiming your sex life, and one that every couple should consider.

Embarking on a major program like this Tantric-based series of exercises requires more decisive measures. You need to get away from everyday circumstances and find somewhere that is quiet, private, and comfortable: quiet so that you can concentrate exclusively on the exercises; private so that there are no distractions, or anxiety to get in the way of the feelings you are trying to express. This will allow you to free your mind from mundane, everyday concerns and focus on sexual and spiritual matters. You need an environment that works with the exercises to promote a mental and spiritual contact with your partner.

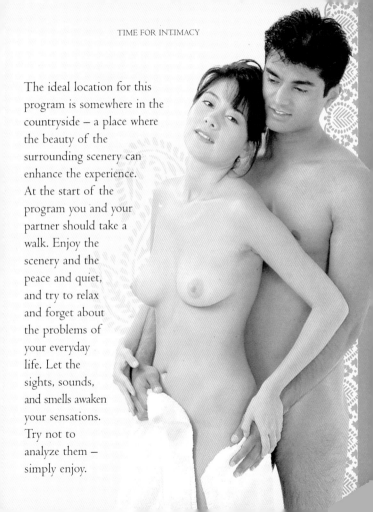

The ideal location for this program is somewhere in the countryside – a place where the beauty of the surrounding scenery can enhance the experience. At the start of the program you and your partner should take a walk. Enjoy the scenery and the peace and quiet, and try to relax and forget about the problems of your everyday life. Let the sights, sounds, and smells awaken your sensations. Try not to analyze them – simply enjoy.

Discarding Stress

Stress is an increasingly common cause of physical and mental illness, but few people realize what wide-ranging consequences it can have. Stress can affect your relationship, your sex drive, and even your ability to become aroused and perform. Women in particular find it hard to experience orgasm when concerned about nagging anxieties. Many of the preliminaries to lovemaking have the effect of relaxing the body, focusing the mind, and helping lovers to leave the cares of the everyday world firmly behind them.

Before you can achieve a union of consciousness with your partner, you must free your mind of distracting influences and rid your body of the debilitating tensions of daily life.

Try incorporating a simple relaxation exercise into your three-day course (especially on the first day, to get into the right frame of mind). Then, should you feel tense or anxious at any time during the program, use the technique as a tool to get yourself back into the right spirit and general frame of mind.

PROGRESSIVE MUSCLE RELAXATION

Find a quiet spot where you can stretch out and feel
comfortable. Lie down on your back with your arms by
your sides, and close your eyes. The aim is to focus on
one muscle group at a time, sensing it and then
relaxing it. Start at your toes (wiggle them first to get a
sense of them), then move on to the sole of your foot,
the top and the ankle. Do the other foot. Then move
on to your calves, shins, thighs, etc. This technique
involves the use of your kinesthetic sense – the sense
whereby each part of your body knows where it is in
space and in relation to each other part. When you get
to your chest, work up your arms from the fingers.
Finish off by working all the way up to your head,
relaxing each part of your face and then trying to
sense your scalp. Visualize it relaxing.

Three-Day Program:
Day One

The first day of the three-day program is a day for getting to know each other. No matter that you may have lived together for ten years: today you will begin to tear aside the veil of privacy that, over the years, you have instinctively but unconsciously placed between yourself and your lover, and will dare to expose yourself without reservation. Spend some time talking, and reminisce about what it was like when you first met. Remember the beauty of your love in the beginning, the way you felt about each other early in your relationship.

When you talk with your partner about yourself and your relationship, let down your defenses and be completely open about your feelings. Don't be afraid to show emotion: hold hands, laugh, cry, and talk freely of your fears, fantasies, hopes, and hates. Speak of anything and everything – but do not say anything that might hurt your partner.

Give each other plenty of time to speak and to express opinions, thoughts, hopes, and fears, and throughout your conversation pay careful attention to

what is being said. Make it obvious to your partner that you are really listening. Try to make each other feel good, and do caring things such as offering each other little gifts.

Although you may hold hands, or walk arm in arm, that is the sole extent of today's touching. Hold back from kissing one another, fondling and making love. In the evening, talk a little more. Share your feelings about this exercise and its progress, and talk about what it is like to be together without making love.

When you go to bed on the first night, kiss if you must, but not deeply, and do not caress. Sleep in each other's arms, but hold back from lovemaking. There is plenty of time ahead in which to make love.

Three-Day Program: Day Two

*A*fter you have bathed and eaten a light breakfast, ensure that you will not be disturbed, and close the doors and windows to your room. Sit opposite each other naked, and close enough to touch easily. Very gently reach forward and begin to stroke each other as lightly and tenderly as possible. Stroke anywhere except the breasts or genitals.

You may become exceedingly aroused, to the extent that you tremble, cry out, or break into a fine sweat. Continue the stroking for half an hour if you can. When you have finished, lie down on your backs, side by side, and relax together to allow the sexual tension to drain away.

When you are both feeling completely relaxed, and the sexual feeling has dispersed from you both, bathe separately in warm water. Then once more sit opposite each other, naked, and commence the stroking exercise for a further quarter of an hour.

Later, eat a light lunch and go for a walk. Hold hands as you walk, and be quiet or talk about your feelings as you choose. If one of you feels that the

exercise is useless and not worth continuing with, just try and enjoy the feelings on your own for the moment, concentrating on what you are aiming to achieve.

In the evening begin the stroking exercise again. Only this time, as you do it, imagine that the touch you are bestowing on your partner can be felt by you. For instance, if you stroke your partner on the arm, imagine it is your own arm that is being stroked and try to think what it would feel like to be touched in that manner.

The point of this exercise is to encourage you, by using your imagination, to experience your partner's feelings rather than your own — to empathize with them. Try to spend at least half an hour on the exercise. Again resist any urge to have sex that night and go to sleep, as on the first night.

Three-Day Program:
Day Three

*B*egin the third and final day of the program with a bath or shower and a light breakfast. As on the second morning, ensure that you have total privacy and carry on with the empathic stroking.

Take your clothes off and sit close together. Once again, stroke each other lightly and tenderly. This time stroke each other all over, including the breasts, labia, vagina, penis, and testicles. The strokes should be as light as you can make them. As before, try not to speak, but allow yourself to moan, gasp, or cry out if your arousal becomes intense.

Empathize with your partner, as on the previous evening, by trying to imagine that you can feel the touches you are giving in the same way that he or she can feel them. Pay particular attention to the touches on the breasts and genitals, because these touches were not part of the empathic stroking exercise that you did before. Keep on with these caresses for about an hour, take a five-minute rest before moving on to of the exercise, which involves penetration.

After the rest, the man should lie flat on his back. Then his partner should sit astride him and gently lower her vagina onto his erect penis. If he does not already have an erection, either he or his partner should masturbate him by hand so that he acquires one.

Once she has inserted his erect penis into her vagina, there should be no more movement from either him or her. She simply sits, then stretches out and lies face-down on top of him, holding his penis within her. Once she has achieved this position she just lies there peacefully, without moving, until the man's erection has subsided. She does not let herself be tempted to move or come to orgasm.

When you have completed this exercise you are ready for the final part of the program, in which you will enjoy full intercourse.

Three-Day Program:
Evening Exercise

Before moving into the final phase of the three-day program, wash, dress, and go for a walk together. Spend the afternoon talking over your thoughts and feelings about the program so far, and discuss the effects it has had on your feelings for each other.

In the evening do the stroking and penetration exercise again for an hour or so, concentrating on the empathic quality of your touch until you feel that you have virtually merged identities with your partner. Now you are ready to complete the program by having uninhibited intercourse.

Aim for a long, slow intercourse in which the man holds back until his partner has reached orgasm. You can even try for simultaneous orgasms using these special Tantric techniques.

Tantric stroking is an Eastern version of Masters and Johnson's "sensate focus." But it is a version that contains an interesting and important difference. The first half of the exercise echoes the "touch for pleasure's sake" principle, but the second moves on to something that is altogether more profound; something capable of touching the spirit as well as the body.

There are two sensations to be appreciated. The first is your own – what you feel when you touch your partner. The second is about developing empathy – you are literally tuning in, through your fingertips, to what your partner is experiencing when touched by you. This second allows your imagination to dwell in your partner's mind – it encourages you to be at your most loving in imagination and skilful with strokes, because this might be your own body presently offered a taste of almost unearthly bliss.

By learning, in this small way, how to "be" your partner, you are also learning a profound lesson in life. The man or woman who can tune into a lover and "read" their thoughts will always be highly valued as an exceptionally loving and caring person.

Quiet Contemplation

We live life at such speed in the 21st century that we have lost sight of the fact that quiet times of contemplation are soothing to the soul. Learning to enjoy what we have in the "here and now" instead of constantly looking forward to the next thing is a skill we appear to be losing. Yet it is important to cultivate the art of reflection, because if we cannot enjoy what happens NOW, there is not a lot of point to anything anymore. Love and sex are no exception to this basic rule of human existence.

It almost sounds rude to advocate that we should take time out to think. There are certainly many who consider thought, or self-analysis, to be self-centered solipsism. Yet without thought, without consideration of who we are and where we are, we live life only in a state of blindness. At the time the *Kama Sutra* was written, men and women would regularly spend a short but quiet time making a "puja" — a short form of prayer. Indeed, many Eastern men and women still do this today. It is a custom that we in the West might benefit from by borrowing.

A Daily Ritual

Instead of embracing aspects of love unthinkingly, dwell quietly for five minutes of each day on one small aspect of sexuality. Turn this contemplation into a small ritual. Withdraw to a quiet room, where you can ensure that there will be no interruptions. Find a focus in the room that you like to look at. Perhaps it is a picture, a porcelain object — even your own reflection in the mirror — but sit quietly in front of it. Relax your shoulders, your body. Relax your mind. Now consider one small sentence about love or sex.

All you have to do is to think about the meaning of the sentence: What is it about? What is its pertinence to you? Do you agree with it? Or disagree? If you agree, how can you use this idea?

Here are a few statements taken from the Sir Richard Burton version of the *Kama Sutra* which I offer as food for thought. Choose your favorite.

"The consciousness of pleasure in men and women is different. The man thinks 'this woman is united with me' and the woman thinks, 'I am united with this man'."

"Woman's passion is marked by her movement in sex. At the beginning of coition her passion is middling but by degrees her passion increases until she ceases to think about her body."

"To the Hindu, sex is a part of his religion, as chastity is part of Christianity. The Hindu looks upon sexual gratification not as mere sensuality, but as a religious act."

"A woman must never permit herself a pleasure with her husband which she has not the skill first to make him desire."

"Love is the creative breath of God."

Safer Sex

Although sexual diseases were already in existence by the time the *Kama Sutra* was written, Vatsyayana makes no mention of them. People have always sought to avoid such infections, but the practice of "safer sex" is a very recent phenomenon. What has prompted this change in sexual behavior is the dramatic spread of AIDS (Acquired Immune Deficiency Syndrome). The term "safer sex" describes sexual activity that is unlikely to expose the participants to infection by HIV (the Human Immunodeficiency Virus), which is the cause of AIDS. The basis of safer sex is to avoid the exchange of bodily fluids, because this exchange is the most common way in which the virus is passed on. The most effective way of minimizing the risk of transmitting HIV infection during intercourse is to use a latex condom with a spermicide containing nonoxynol-9.

MINIMIZING RISK

When complete trust exists between partners, and each is confident enough of the other's sexual history to be reasonably sure that there is no risk of HIV infection, safer sex is irrelevant. But there is always the risk that any new partner will be infected. New partners should always practice safer sex. Blood tests for exposure to HIV can serve as an indicator that infection is unlikely.

NON-PENETRATIVE SEX

As sensitive lovers know, penetration need not occur every time a couple has sex. Dry kissing, embracing, stroking, and massage all express closeness with minimal risk of HIV infection. Mutual masturbation may be used in the same way, but to be extra safe, the partners should try to stop any semen or vaginal fluid from coming into contact with their fingers or hands in case there are any abrasions, or open sores on them.

Oral sex is a high-risk activity, particularly if the bodily fluids it produces are swallowed. A degree of protection is provided by using a condom during fellatio and a latex barrier ("dental dam") during cunnilingus, although neither method is totally safe.

In accepting non-penetrative sexual activities as a valuable part of their relationship, men and women who have any reason to suspect that they might transmit the virus to each other will come to rely less on coital sex. When intercourse does take place, they should always use a condom.

HIV and the Development of AIDS

When HIV gets into the bloodstream, it attacks the immune system, the complex mechanism that enables the body to defend itself against disease. This damage eventually leaves the body vulnerable to other infections and liable to contract otherwise rare illnesses. When a person with HIV begins to be affected by such illnesses, he or she is said to have developed AIDS.

When a person is infected with HIV, the virus will be present in his or her blood. It will also be present in the semen of infected males and in the vaginal secretions of infected females. Anyone coming into intimate contact with these infected bodily fluids will be at high risk of contracting the virus themselves.

The condom plays a central role in the practice of safer sex. Not only does it substantially reduce the risk of HIV infection, it also offers effective protection against other sexually transmitted diseases. The main objections to the use of condoms are that putting them on interrupts the flow of lovemaking and that they reduce sensation for the man. The answer to the first problem is to get into the habit of making the task an erotic experience for both partners and part of foreplay. The second objection is to some extent valid, but in any case, some loss of sensation is surely a small price to pay for protection against HIV and other infections, including syphilis and herpes.

Prolonging the Mood

Partners who genuinely care for each other will want to prolong the unique closeness that lovemaking brings by staying close emotionally and physically. Having just reaffirmed a continuing intimate bond, some couples find that after making love they can talk more easily about things that matter to them either as a couple or as individuals. It is important to be able to communicate what you enjoy most about your sexual relationship, and indeed to feel free to tell your partner if there is anything about your lovemaking that you would like to change. Some couples talk about these things while making love, while others find it easier afterward, as they look back on the pleasures, and the occasional disappointments, they have shared. Often, though, a couple will want to resume their lovemaking, in which case it might be necessary for the woman to masturbate the man to get him erect again. If they

do not intend to make love again, but the woman was not able to reach a satisfactory climax, the considerate thing for the man to do would be to masturbate his partner to help her achieve orgasm.

Most lovers do not want to dissipate the warm glow of lovemaking by simply turning over and going to sleep, or by doing anything that is in any way too demanding. Some simply like to lie quietly in each other's arms, while others prefer to follow love with gentle stroking. If they choose to get up, they may want to sustain the relaxed, harmonious mood by eating together, or enjoying an undemanding activity such as listening to music or taking a leisurely walk.

Index

A

AIDS 230–3
Ananga Ranga positions
    140–81
  Accomplishing 166–7
  Ascending 180
  Crab embrace 156–7
  Crying out 176–7
  Encircling 154
  Equals, of 168–9
  Gaping 152–3
  Intact posture 150
  Inverted embrace 181
  Kama's wheel 148–9
  Level feet posture 144–5
  Lotus 164–5
  Orgasmic role-reversal
    178–9
  Paired feet 174–5
  Placid embrace 151
  Raised feet posture 146
  Refined posture 147
  Snake trap 172–3
  Splitting 155
  Transverse lute 158–9

B

Before and after love
    210–36
Biting 68–9
  'Broken cloud' bite 68
  'of a boar' 69

C

Choosing a mate 14–15
Creating confidence in the
  man 102–3
Creating confidence in the
  woman 104–5
Creating the mood 30–1
Cunnilingus 70–1

D E F

Dating 18–19
Embraces
  Milk and water 40–1
  Twining of a creeper
    38–9
Embracing love 36–7
Erogenous zones 26–9
Fellatio 74–5

G

Getting close to your partner
212–13
Grooming 42–3

H I

Hair play 52–3
HIV infection 230–3
Imagination, power of the
138–9
Intimacy, time for 214–15

K L

Kama Sutra positions 78–139
    Clasping 94–5
    Congress of a cow
    136–7
    Crab's 118–19
    Elephant posture
    134–5
    Fixing of a nail 115
    Half-pressed 110–11
    Lotus-like 116–17
    Mare's 106–7
    Pair of tongs 132–3
    Pressed 112–13
    Pressing 98–9
    Rising 108–9

Kama Sutra positions (cont.)
    Side-by-side clasping
    96–7
    Splitting of a bamboo
    114
    Supported congress
    126–7
    Suspended congress
    124–5
    Swing, the 130–1
    Top, the 128–9
    Turning 120–3
    Twining 100–1
    Variant yawning 84–5
    Widely opened 86–7
    Wife of Indra 88–9
    Yawning 82–3
Kissing 54–77
    and licking 66–7
    Bent kiss 59
    body, the 64–5
    Congress of a crow
    76–7
    Nominal kiss 63
    sensual 58–9
    Straight kiss 58
    Throbbing kiss 63
    Touching kiss 63

L

Letting yourself go 139
Licking 66–7
Love and marriage 16

M

Man's duty to his partner
    90–1
Massage 44–9
    basic massage strokes
        46–7
    sensual massage
        44–5, 48–9
    creating 42
Men, Three Orders of
    162–3
Mood, prolonging 234–6
Mutual grooming 42–3

O P Q

Oral pleasure 72–3
Orgasms, multiple 170–1
Perfumed Garden positions
    182–209
    Eighth posture 202–3
    Eleventh posture 208–9
    Fifth posture 194–5
    First posture 186–7

Perfumed Garden positions (cont.)
    Fourth posture 192–3
    movements of love
        196–7
    Ninth posture 204–5
    Second posture 188–9
    Seventh posture 200–1
    Sixth posture 198–9
    Tenth posture 206–7
    Third posture 190–1
Playing the kissing game
    62–3
Preparing for love 12–33
Preparing the body 24–5
Preparing the mind 22–3
Quiet contemplation
    226–9

R S

Relaxation 216–17
Safer sex 230–3
Scratching 50–1
Sensual kissing 58–9
Setting for love, the 32–3
Sex and caste 20
Sexual equality 93
Social behavior 20–1
Stress, discarding 216–17